Harriet and the Robot

Harriet and the Robot

By Martin Waddell

Illustrated by
Mark Burgess

Joy Street Books
Little, Brown and Company
Boston   Toronto

First American Edition

Library of Congress Cataloging-in-Publication Data
Waddell, Martin.
   Harriet and the robot.

   Summary: Harriet, who brings TROUBLE wherever
she goes, gives her dear friend Anthea a doll for her
birthday — a large robot she has made herself and is not
quite able to control.
   [1. Robots — Fiction. 2. Schools — Fiction]
I. Burgess, Mark, ill. II. Title.
PZ7.W1137Har 1987   [Fic]   86-17435
ISBN 0-316-91624-2

RRD-VA

Printed in the United States of America

A book for
Tara Carragher

Contents

Harriet
and the
Robot

1 | Harriet and the Surprise

"Three hundred and sixty-three days gone!" said Anthea importantly. "One day to go! And this is it!"

"What is it?" said Harriet. The two girls were on their way home from Slow Street School.

"Today is it!" said Anthea. "Tuesday. The day before my birthday!"

"Your birthday?" frowned Harriet. "Oh dear!"

"Oh dear what?" said Anthea.

"I . . . er . . ." said Harriet, thinking quickly. She needed to change the subject. She had forgotten about Anthea's birthday, and Harriet *never* forgot birthdays. She liked birthdays, because she liked giving people she loved Big Surprises to make them happy. The Big Surprises didn't always work out, but Harriet always tried very hard.

"I . . . er . . . I want to walk home past the park."

"Let's go *through* the park," said Anthea agreeably.

"Can't," said Harriet. "I'm barred from the park."

"Why?" said Anthea.

"I had a nice picnic with my Mother and Dad," Harriet said.

"People don't get barred from the park for having nice picnics," said Anthea slowly. "Are you sure you are barred?"

"That's what the Fire Chief said," answered Harriet.

Anthea thought about it.

"What did you set fire to?" she asked, as they turned the corner of Harriet's street.

"Only the bandstand," said Harriet.

"*Why* did you set fire to the bandstand, Harriet?" Anthea asked.

"Dad said I could light the picnic fire," said Harriet. "It was only a little one, so we could cook our hamburgers. It was windy, so I thought I'd use the bandstand for a windbreak, and the wind changed, and the fire sort of blew . . . Anyway, it was a rotten band."

"What was?" said Anthea.

"The band that was on the bandstand when I burned it down," said Harriet. "They made an awful noise jumping off."

"You burned down the bandstand with a band playing on it?" said Anthea.

"I didn't *mean* to," said Harriet, and then she added brightly, "I didn't burn the hamburgers. They were delicious. Perhaps . . . perhaps I could give you a Big Surprise picnic on the common, for your birthday?"

"I think you'd better not, Harriet," said Anthea hurriedly. "Anyway, I don't *want* a birthday picnic! I want a birthday *present!*"

"Y-e-s," said Harriet. "Only there isn't much time, is there, if your birthday is tomorrow?"

"I hope I'll get lots of presents," said Anthea cheerfully. "You'll give me something nice this time, Harriet, won't you, not like last time?"

Harriet looked hurt. "I gave you a rhinoceros," she said. "Didn't you like it?"

"Not really," said Anthea, and then she spotted the look on Harriet's face. "Not too well," she amended. "It was rough to play with, wasn't it?"

"Most rhinoceroses are," Harriet pointed out.

"Most real ones are," said Anthea. "I didn't want a *real* one. I wanted a plastic one, for my toy zoo."

"It did charge nicely, though, didn't it?" said Harriet. "Chasing all those policemen! I wonder where it ended up."

Anthea didn't say anything. She didn't *want* to know where her lost rhinoceros was. She didn't think Harriet should have given her a real one in the first place, and Harriet certainly shouldn't have taken it walking in the park, on a piece of string.

"Something *nice*, this time, Harriet," said

6

Anthea. "Like . . . like a doll. I'd *like* a doll."

"You've got a doll," said Harriet scornfully. "You've got hundreds! They're hopeless, they don't do anything."

"My best doll says 'Ma-ma,' " said Anthea proudly. Anthea's best doll was called Florence, after her Auntie. She wanted to call it "Harriet," because Harriet was her best friend, but her Mum wouldn't allow it. Mum said the name "Harriet" reminded her of things she'd rather not think about.

"A doll," said Harriet thoughtfully. "We'll see."

"Mother?" said Harriet.

"Yes dear?" said Mrs. Smith.

"Dolls are boring, aren't they, Mother?"

"I suppose so, dear, for a big girl like you."

"What about for a little girl like Anthea?" said Harriet. "For her birthday?"

"Sounds very nice, dear," said Mrs. Smith.

"Y-e-s," said Harriet doubtfully. "Only . . . only Anthea's my best friend, and she didn't like the rhinoceros I gave her last year, and this year . . . this year I'd like to give her something Extra Special nice, to make up for it."

"How about an Extra Special Doll?" said Mrs. Smith. "A doll who could do things?"

"What sort of things?" said Harriet.

"Useful things," said Mrs. Smith brightly.

Harriet went away to think about it, and then she got out her bike and buzzed down to the library.

"Ma'am?" said Harriet.

"Yes, Harriet?" said Mrs. Yeo, the Librarian, warily.

"Can I have my rope, please, Ma'am," said Harriet politely.

"Of course, dear," said Mrs. Yeo, and she took out the rope and attached one end to Harriet, and one end to the desk. The rope was to stop Harriet from doing things. It was a Library Rule for the Admission of Harriet, as a Safety Precaution.

"I want a book on computers, please," said Harriet. "On computers making things move!"

"What sort of things?" Mrs. Yeo asked nervously.

8

"A do . . . just *things*," said Harriet. And then she added, "I can't tell you, because it is going to be a Big Surprise for Someone I'm Extra Special fond of!

"Not me?" said Mrs. Yeo.

"Not you," said Harriet. "Although I'm Extra Special fond of you too, for arranging about my rope. If it hadn't been for you, I wouldn't have been allowed in here again, would I?"

"Not after they rebuilt the library," said Mrs. Yeo.

She gave Harriet a book on computers, and Harriet went to the library table, where she sat down and started working.

"What's Harriet *doing?*" said Sylvester Wise.

Sylvester was Harriet's Chief Rival at Slow Street School, and the Head of the Anti-Harriet League. That is why he was crouched behind the old books, pretending to be a pile of encyclopedias. It was his turn for Harriet Surveillance. The Anti-Harriet League was on almost constant Harriet Surveillance. It was the Price of Their Survival. They did it very carefully, and in pairs.

"I don't want to know," shivered Fat Olga. She was standing in the rubber-plant container, trying to look like a rubber plant.

Sylvester Wise was made of sterner stuff.

"She's drawing something," he reported. "Something big. On graph paper. With colored pencils. She keeps stopping, and checking the book, and tearing the graph paper up, and looking again and drawing and. . . ."

"I want to go home," said the rubber plant.

"Plans!" said Sylvester, paying no attention. "Inventing something!"

"What for?" said the rubber plant.

"Bashing us, probably," said Sylvester glumly.

"Oh Mummy!" groaned the rubber plant.

When Harriet left the library, Fat Olga and Sylvester were close behind.

Harriet went in and out of several shops, and on the way she acquired a large plastic bag, which got fuller and fuller and fuller.

"What's she doing?" moaned Fat Olga.

"Don't know," said Sylvester.

"Then we're doomed!" said Fat Olga.

"Probably," said Sylvester wisely.

It was his last word on the subject, but it wasn't his last action. Sylvester's Super Brain whirred into motion. It didn't come up with anything, but it whirred, and kept on whirring into the long hours of the night.

In any other school but Slow Street, Sylvester would have been the Children's Champion, and a Hero. In Slow Street he was One of the Oppressed.

That was because of Harriet.

But Sylvester was determined to change things, just for once.

For twice was too much to hope for.

2 | The Secret Laboratory

There was a sign outside Harriet's room.

SECRET LABORATORY
EXPERIMENTS IN PROGRESS
KEEP OUT.

(SIGNED)
H Smith

Mr. and Mrs. Smith were worried. They knew that H. SMITH stood for Harriet, but they didn't know what the zizzes and clunks and clinks coming from behind the door stood for, or why Harriet had locked herself in.

"Harriet, dear! Supper!" Mrs. Smith called.

"Oh bother!" said Harriet's voice, through the door. "Down in a minute, Mother!"

Mrs. Smith went back downstairs.

Harriet came down, five minutes later.

She was wearing a sun hat, although it was midwinter.

"Dig in, Harriet," said Mr. Smith cheerfully.

Mr. and Mrs. Smith were having tea and toast, because they were very small people, and never ate a lot. Harriet was having Coke and ham sandwiches and a cheeseburger and three sausages and french fries, double helping, because she was a growing girl.

"Why are you wearing your sun hat, Harriet dear?" Mrs. Smith asked, halfway through the meal.

"I had a little accident," said Harriet. "Not *really* an accident at all. Just a *little* one, very little."

"What sort of an accident?" asked Mr. Smith. "I hope you haven't hurt yourself, dear?"

Harriet took off her sun hat.

"Oh, Harriet!" said Mrs. Smith in dismay.

"I think short, singed hair suits her," said Mr. Smith brightly.

After supper, Anthea came over to play.

"You're all baldy, Harriet," she said.

"No I'm not," said Harriet.

"Hair feeds the brain," said Anthea. "I expect your brain won't get fed, and you will shrivel up and die."

"What about all the bald people?" asked Harriet. "They don't shrivel up and die, do they?"

"They get used to it, I expect," said Anthea. "How did you get your hair singed, Harriet?"

"Experimenting," said Harriet importantly.

"What with?" said Anthea. "Not . . . not dynamite *again?*"

"My Dad won't let me have any more dynamite," said Harriet indignantly.

"It was a very big hole you blew in the ship," Anthea pointed out. "I don't blame him."

"I didn't mean to sink the ship," Harriet said. "Little mistakes like that happen to Inventors."

"Are you inventing something, Harriet?" Anthea asked nervously.

"Yes," said Harriet. "It's a Big-Surprise-for-Somebody-I-Like's-Birthday and I'm not saying any more about it until after the Test Run."

Anthea thought about it.

"Is the *somebody* ME, Harriet?" she asked.

"Yes!" said Harriet.

"Oh goody!" said Anthea, and she skipped off home to tell her Mum about the Big Birthday Surprise, and the Test Run.

"When is the Test Run?" asked Anthea's Mum.

"Harriet said tonight," said Anthea. "So my Big Surprise will be ready for my birthday."

Anthea's Mum locked all the doors and windows and kept the cat in. She went to bed with a baseball bat and a book on Controlling Wild Animals, just in case.

The moon glistened on the snow in the Slow Street School Playground as Harriet pushed her wheelbarrow through the gates.

The Test Run began.

"ONE-TWO-THREE . . . GO!"

Nothing happened.

Harriet punched again at the remote-control unit. It was from the Smiths' TV set and it usually worked fine at home, but this time it didn't seem to be working at all.

"Bother!" said Harriet. "It's supposed to be One for Go, Two for Turn Left, Three for Turn Right, Four for Stop, but it won't work!"

She got out her screwdriver, and started making adjustments.

Then . . .

"ONE-TWO-THREE . . . GO!" Harriet pressed the remote-control unit and, this time . . .

Creak-squeak-creak

"YIPPEE!"

The Big Surprise lumbered across the playground, with Harriet walking behind it, heading for the fence.

Harriet pressed Two for Turn Left.

The Big Surprise paid no attention.

Harriet pressed Three for Turn Right.

The Big Surprise smashed into the fence, which shattered under the impact.

"STOP!" yelled Harriet, wildly pressing Four, but the Big Surprise didn't stop.

It marched through the fence, and across the road, and BONG!

"Silly lamppost!" said Harriet, and tried to straighten it, but she couldn't, because the lamppost was very bent.

So was the Big Surprise.

Oil was running out of its rubber joints, all over the road.

"Not quite right *yet*," muttered Harriet, and she fetched her wheelbarrow through the hole in the fence and collected the Big Surprise, and the little bits of the Big Surprise that had fallen off.

She wheeled it all home, and went straight up to her Secret Laboratory to continue Testing, leaving the TV remote-control unit downstairs, since it didn't seem to be working anyway.

Harriet began a new set of experiments, this time using sound control.

She went *"Peeep"* and *"Peeep-Peeep-Peeeeep"* and *"Peeep Peeep"* and *"Peeeeep Pep Peep!"* with her Special Whistle.

"Brilliant!" breathed Harriet.

More work, and more *peeps*, and "GREAT!" said Harriet.

"SUPER!"

"FANTABOLOUS!"

It was half-past midnight. Anthea was fast asleep. The Anti-Harriet League were tucked up in their beds, having nightmares about Harriet. Mr. and Mrs. Smith were snoring gently. Almost the whole town had gone to sleep, except for the Emergency Light Repairs Service, which was busy lamppost-rebending on Slow Street, which was difficult because of all the oil underfoot.

Then . . .

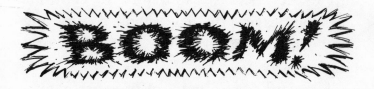

Mrs. Smith was blown straight out of bed and across the landing and into the bathroom, where she ended up sitting in the bath on top of Harriet's rubber python.

Mr. Smith blew the other way, down the stairs. He had gone to bed wearing his Harriet-Is-at-Work Safety Kit, as a precaution. The strap of his Kit caught on a coat hook, and he swung there like a pendulum, moving gently to and fro in the breeze that was coming from where the front door used to be.

The front door was across the street, in

Mr. Goodbody's house, where it gave him a nasty shock in the morning.

Black smoke blew everywhere, mingling with clouds of plaster dust.

A figure emerged from roughly the place where the Secret Laboratory used to be.

"Mother!" Harriet shouted excitedly. "Mother! Dad! *It's working!*"

3 | A Reign of Terror?

A spread of soft snow covered Mitford, and all was bright and beautiful on a cold, clear morning as two happy feet crunched down Harriet's street, and a little voice trilled an excited song:

"Happy Birthday to me
Happy Birthday to me
Happy Birthday, Dear Anthea
Happy Birthday to me!"

It was Anthea in her new birthday coat, carrying her birthday muff, still in its box. It wasn't cold enough to wear it, but she wanted to show it to Harriet.

She stopped trilling outside the gate of Harriet's house.

Harriet's house had a hole in the roof, and no windows, and a grandfather clock with its works removed lying among what was left of the furniture in the front garden.

"Harriet?" Anthea called, peering anxiously through the bit of the gate that was still held on by the hinges.

No one answered. Nothing stirred, except for a thin plume of smoke rising from behind the house.

Anthea stepped cautiously through the hole where the rest of the gate had been and tiptoed down the path. She followed the trail of smoke, which led her to the back garden. Harriet was standing beside a small bonfire, made up of pieces of broken stair-case. It was blazing brightly, and melting the snow on Harriet's snowmen.

"You're standing too close to that fire, Harriet," said Anthea, standing well back, because she didn't want to get soot on her birthday coat.

"No, I'm not," said Harriet.

"Yes, you are," said Anthea. "You look all brown, and sort of smoky."

"Do I?" said Harriet, stifling a yawn.

"And your house looks as if it has been blown up *again*," said Anthea, looking around for her present. She was beginning to wonder if the Big Surprise had been blown up too.

"It's only a bit blown up this time," said Harriet, piling more of the staircase onto the fire. "My Dad will fix it." She was very proud of her Dad's fixing. He was good at it because he got a lot of practice.

"Ah-hem!" said Anthea, spinning around to show off her new coat. "Look at me, Harriet! Look at my birthday coat. Look at my new muff! My Mum gave them to me."

"Oh! Super!" said Harriet, admiringly. "Happy Birthday, Anthea!"

"Happy Birthday!" said another voice.

Anthea jumped. She hadn't realized that

Mrs. Smith was in the garden. She turned around to show Mrs. Smith her coat and muff, but she couldn't see her. The only things she saw in the garden were Harriet's snowmen, sitting in their deck chairs around the fire.

Then one of Harriet's snowmen spoke to her.

It said, "What a lovely little coat, Anthea! You are a lucky girl," in Mrs. Smith's voice.

"*Aaaaaaaah!*" screamed Anthea, backing away.

"Careful, Anthea!" said the other snow-man, in Mr. Smith's voice.

"They . . . they *spoke!*" squeaked Anthea. "They spoke to me!"

"Mothers and Dads do," said Harriet sensibly. She thought they spoke too much, most of the time.

"But . . . but they're snowmen!" said Anthea.

"They're not snowmen," said Harriet. "Snowmen don't sit around in deck chairs, do they?"

"But . . ."

"This one is my Mother, and this is my Dad," said Harriet. "At least I think so. It *is* a bit difficult to tell them apart, because of the snow. I expect I'll recognize them a bit better when they've melted."

"Melted?" said Anthea.

"They've been out all night in the garden," Harriet explained. "Since I blew up the house. They felt safer being outside what was left."

Anthea considered for a moment, and then she asked:

"Why did you blow up your house, Harriet?"

"I didn't *mean* to blow it up," Harriet explained. "I was doing something else."

"What were you doing, Harriet?" Anthea asked.

"It's a Big Surprise for someone I'm Extra Special fond of!" Harriet said. "Somebody whose birthday this just happens to be."

There was a long silence.

"You blew up your house for my birthday?" Anthea said. She was used to Harriet's house being blown up. She didn't think much of it as a Big Surprise.

"Come with me to the garage!" said Harriet proudly.

Anthea came after her, slowly.

"Now close your eyes and count to ten!" Harriet ordered.

"Is it . . . is it safe, Harriet?" Anthea asked.

"CLOSE YOUR EYES!" ordered Harriet.

Anthea closed her eyes.

"One-two-three-four-five-six-seven-eight-nine-ten . . ."

"HAPPY BIRTHDAY, ANTHEA!" shouted Harriet.

Anthea opened her eyes.

"*Ooooooh!*" she said, and she clapped her hands and skipped with excitement. "Oh! Harriet! Super! A Big Dolly! My Biggest Dolly ever!"

"It's not just a Big Dolly," said Harriet scornfully. "It's a Robot. Your own Robot. Specially for you!"

"A *what?*" said Anthea.

"My Special Whistle works it," said Harriet, and she blew her Special Whistle softly. "*Peep.*"

"It moved!" shrieked Anthea. "My Big Dolly moved!"

"*Peep-Peep.*"

The Robot turned toward Anthea.

"Ug," it said.

"I'm still working on the talking," said Harriet. "It is very clever otherwise. It can spell and do math with its computer brain."

"*Peep-peep-peep-peep,*" went Harriet, and the Robot stopped moving.

"It's . . . it's . . . *she's* very nice, Harriet," said Anthea.

"And useful," Harriet pointed out.

"I shall call her Dolly," said Anthea.

"It is the smartest Robot ever," said Harriet. "Let's take it to school today so that it can do all our math and spelling and things and we'll be the best in the class."

"I usually am, anyway," said Anthea.

"Well I'm not," said Harriet, who had more interesting things to do than lessons. "I bet nobody else in our school ever made a Robot of their very own."

"Who else would?" wondered Anthea, and the three of them set off for school.

First they came to the trash can at what was left of Harriet's gate. It hadn't been there when Anthea arrived. She stopped and looked at it suspiciously.

"Harriet . . . ?" she said.

Harriet lifted the lid.

"Good morning, Sylvester," she said.

"Goo . . ." Sylvester began, but then

Harriet put the lid down firmly on his nose.

"Well done, Anthea!" said Harriet, and they clicked off down the road.

Harriet and Anthea weren't clicking, but Dolly was.

The Anti-Harriet League's Surveillance Trash Can followed at a discreet distance. It had no bottom, because that was where Sylvester's feet and legs came out. It had two eyeholes in the lid and just enough space for Sylvester inside.

The group he was following came to an icy patch.

Dolly stopped. The computer brain inside her head didn't like the look of the ice.

"Copy Mode!" said Harriet. She gave two short *peeps* and a long one, and then she jumped over the patch.

"Ug!" said Dolly. She jumped over the icy patch, skidded, and sat down.

"I haven't got that Copy Mode quite right yet," said Harriet fretfully. "But I'm working on it."

"Poor Dolly," said Anthea, helping her to her feet.

"Ug," said Dolly, shaking her cold bottom.

Anthea and Harriet and Dolly continued down the road.

When Harriet's right leg moved, Dolly's right leg moved, and when Harriet's left leg moved, Dolly's left leg moved, and when Harriet blew her nose, Dolly blew hers.

"Working well now, don't you think?" Harriet said to Anthea.

"Yes," said Anthea. "But my Dolly *clicks* a lot, doesn't she?"

"Only a bit," said Harriet. "I'll oil her when we get to school."

Click-click-click-click!

The clicking worried Sylvester, still concealed in the Anti-Harriet League's Surveillance Trash Can.

There was something odd about the big new girl who was walking behind Harriet, but Sylvester couldn't figure out what it was.

The eyeholes were too small to let him see the big girl very well, and he was too far away to hear the conversation, but close enough to hear the *peeeps* when Harriet gave Dolly fresh instructions.

Sylvester kept following at a distance. He hoped it was a *safe* distance, but you could never be sure with Harriet.

Harriet, Anthea, and Dolly turned in through the school gates.

Charlie Green fled.

Marky Brown hid.

Fat Olga crouched in the bicycle shed, hoping she would be mistaken for a large Schwinn.

Sylvester stopped at the gates and peered around them, to see if the coast was clear.

Somebody tapped on the can's lid.

Sylvester froze.

Somebody lifted the can's lid.

It was Mr. Tiger, the pride of Slow Street School. He looked down into the can, at Sylvester crouching inside, with his feet coming out the bottom.

"Good morning, Wise," he said.

"Good morning, sir," said Sylvester.

Mr. Tiger considered the trash can, with Sylvester inside it. He was a very kind old schoolteacher, the Rock on which the school was built, and had spent many years at Slow Street. He didn't have to ask *why* Sylvester was in the trash can, but he did.

"*Harriet?*" he said.

"Yes, sir," said Sylvester.

"Did she put you in, or are you there of your own accord?" he asked.

"Just sort of hiding, sir," said Sylvester.

"Very sensible, my boy," said Mr. Tiger, and he went off to the Staff Room, with no more questions asked.

Sylvester climbed out of the can and gave the Harriet All-Clear Signal. The rest of the Anti-Harriet League reappeared from their hiding places.

"Now there's going to be *three* of them!" said Fat Olga, wheeling herself out of the shed, and then remembering that she wasn't pretending to be a Schwinn anymore.

"Two and a half," said Marky Brown. "Anthea doesn't count. Not as a whole, anyway."

"That new girl looks very *big*," said Charlie Green.

"It isn't just size that counts," said Fat Olga shrewdly.

"Doesn't hurt, though," muttered Charlie.

The new girl *was* big. Much bigger than Roberta Haynes, even. So big that she was almost unpunchable.

"Harriet and a Big One like that," muttered Fat Olga.

"A Reign of Terror!" said Sylvester darkly, and no one disagreed.

4 | "UG!"

Somebody was screaming.

Miss Granston wasn't the Principal of Slow Street School for nothing. She was Principal because she stood for all that was good and fine and pure in Slow Street. She could not stand idly by while her Staff screamed.

She acted at once. She hid under her desk, put her hands over her ears, and tried to think positively.

It was Mrs. Whitten, the P3 Teacher, who was screaming.

She was lying in the corridor outside the Girls' Cloakroom, under a pile of rubble.

"Help! Help!" she cried.

"Have no fear, help is here!" said Mr. Tiger, calmly pulling her to her feet. Then he stopped, impressed by his own poetry. It was not often that Mr. Tiger's Poetic Muse struck, and when it did he couldn't help admiring it.

"Have no fear,
Help is here,"

he repeated, and then he added, triumphantly,

"You're all right,
But you're all white!"

"Shut up!" said Mrs. Whitten. "Stop reciting! I can't hear myself scream!"

And she screamed again. She was never one to be done out of a good scream, even if she was covered with cement and plaster dust.

"Stop!" commanded Mr. Tiger. "We must ascertain what has occurred!"

"The wall fell down on top of me," said

Mrs. Whitten. "*That* is what has occurred. And I'll stop screaming when I feel like it, not when you say so!"

And she screamed again.

"I see," said Mr. Tiger, sucking on his pipe.

"I see,
Ah me!"

"What do you see?" said Mrs. Whitten.

"A hole in the wall," said Mr. Tiger.

"I've already seen that," said Mrs. Whitten.

"A girl-shaped hole in the wall!" said Mr. Tiger, inspecting it. "Distinctly girl-shaped. As if somebody had meant to walk through the Cloakroom door, and walked through the wall instead!"

"This Copy Mode is going to get us into trouble, Harriet," said Anthea anxiously.

They were down in the boiler room, oiling Dolly so that she wouldn't click so much.

"The door should have been bigger," said Harriet. "It wasn't Dolly's fault."

"I don't *mind* about the door," said Anthea.

"All right," said Harriet. "I know. But Dolly didn't *mean* to hang you up on the coatrack. She just saw me hang my coat up, and you were next to her and. . . ."

"She hung me up," said Anthea, pouting. Anthea wasn't used to hanging from coatracks.

"Say 'Sorry,' Dolly," said Harriet, and she *peeped* softly on her whistle.

"Ug," said Dolly.

"She *means* 'Sorry,' " explained Harriet. "I just haven't got the talking right."

"Never mind," said Anthea. "Don't you think . . . don't you think we should switch Dolly off, and leave her here until school is over?"

"Wait till you see how she spells!" said Harriet. "She's already done my spelling homework."

"A new girl!" said Miss Wilson brightly. "What is your name, dear?"

"Ug," said the new girl.

"Ug?" said Miss Wilson.

"Ug," confirmed the new girl.

"Well, that *is* a pretty name!" said Miss Wilson.

"Pretty unusual!" muttered Sylvester Wise.

"I do hope you'll be happy here, Ug," said Miss Wilson, and the new girl clicked back toward her desk.

"Now, children, *homework*," said Miss Wilson. "Harriet?"

Harriet handed in her homework confidently.

Miss Wilson looked at it, and then frowned.

WEDDNESDAY
THURSDEY
FRYDAY
SOTTERDAY

"It's all *wrong*, Harriet," she said. "As usual."

"But *Miss* . . ." Harriet protested.

"Again!" said Miss Wilson. "Do it again for tomorrow."

Harriet went back to her seat.

On her way, she accidently kicked Dolly, who had the seat in front of her.

And Dolly kicked Fat Olga.

It was definitely a copy-kick.

"I love my Dolly, Harriet," said Anthea. "I really do. I like her just the way she is. I don't mind if she can't spell."

"She *can* spell!" muttered Harriet.

They were back in the boiler room, and Harriet was working on Dolly's insides. There was a lot of bleeping and buzzing and clicking going on, as Harriet adjusted the circuits.

"I don't think T-H-U-R-S-D-E-Y spells 'Thursday,' Harriet," said Anthea. "And F-R-Y-D-A-Y doesn't spell 'Friday.' I'm *almost* certain that Miss Wilson spells them differently. . . ."

"I know that *now*," said Harriet.

"My other dollies can't spell either, Harriet," said Anthea. "I don't mind. I love them just the same. My rhino couldn't spell. . . ."

"You didn't like your rhino," said Harriet accusingly.

42

"I only didn't like it a little bit," said Anthea hopelessly. She did like her Big Dolly, very much. It was the Biggest Dolly she'd ever seen, and a real Big Birthday Surprise. She didn't want her Dolly to be ruined.

"It's only a slight malfunction in the Morse Code Transmitter," said Harriet. "I'm working on it."

"Do be careful with my Dolly, Harriet," Anthea said.

"Of course I'll be careful," said Harriet. "I'm always careful, aren't I?"

"Where are they?" whispered Fat Olga.

"In the boiler room," said Sylvester.

"Doing what?" said Fat Olga.

"Going *click-click* and *peep-peep*," said Sylvester, in a puzzled voice.

They were hiding in the big closet, down the corridor from the boiler room, on Anti-Harriet Surveillance.

"The door is opening," Sylvester hissed, and he pulled the closet door closed so that Harriet and Anthea and the new girl wouldn't see them. He watched Harriet and Anthea and the new girl go down the corridor.

Harriet said: "I'll get all my math right after recess, you wait and see!"

"Y-e-s!" said Anthea doubtfully.

"Won't I, Dolly?" said Harriet.

"Ug!" said Dolly.

Sylvester, crouched inside the closet, frowned.

When the coast was clear, he came out of the closet, clutching his Anti-Harriet Surveillance Notebook.

It had a heading: CLUES TO WHAT HARRIET IS UP TO.

And beneath the heading Sylvester had written:

> The New Girl
> Clicks
> Buzzes
> Peeps
> Says only "Ug."

That was as far as he had gotten into the Mystery. He didn't know about the hole in the school fence or the bent lamppost or the oil slick in the road or the new girl-shaped entrance to the Girls' Cloakroom. If he had known, he might have worked it out. If he had worked it out he might . . . but Sylvester's life was like that — very iffy.

Especially when Harriet was involved.

Miss Wilson crept down the corridor, hoping to make it to the Staff Room in one piece.

She had had a bad morning.

For once, it wasn't Harriet. It was the new girl toward the back of the class. Miss Wilson had tried being nice to her, but the new girl wasn't very cooperative.

She just sat there, saying, "Ug" and "Ug-Ug," and once, in a *very* talkative mood, "Ug-Ug-Ug." It was more than a sensitive teacher could be expected to bear.

"Hello, Miss Wilson!" said Harriet.

Miss Wilson froze.

It was an *ambush*.

It had to be. Three of them, appearing from nowhere, and two of the three were the worst possible two, from Miss Wilson's point of view. Harriet and . . . and . . .

"Hello, girls," said Miss Wilson bravely.

"Ug," said the new girl.

"Ug isn't her *real* name, Miss Wilson," said Harriet. "Her real name is Dolly. She's my . . .

"*Cousin*," said Anthea quickly. "Harriet's Cousin Dolly."

"Ug," agreed Harriet's cousin.

Miss Wilson began to tremble. A new girl who said only 'Ug" was bad enough, but a new girl who was Harriet's cousin. . . .

"Wel . . . welcome to Slow Street, Dolly Ug," she stuttered, and reached out to shake Harriet's cousin's hand.

It was a mistake.

Harriet's cousin's hand came off.

"AAAAAAAAAAAH!" shrieked Miss Wilson.

"Bother," said Harriet. "Another screw loose somewhere."

"AAAAAAAAAH! AAAAAAAAH!" Miss Wilson fled down the corridor, screaming.

"What a big fuss about nothing," Harriet said grumpily.

Miss Granston was trapped. She should have been safely in her office with the Tonic Wine, but she wasn't.

She was in the Staff Room when the screaming started, and now there was no escape.

She tiptoed to the Staff Room door and looked out.

Mr. Tiger was coming down the corridor.

"Good morning, Mr. Tiger," she said. "Did you scream?"

"Nope," said Mr. Tiger, puffing cheerfully on his pipe.

"AAAAAAAAAAAH!" the scream echoed around them.

"It's only Miss Wilson *again*," said Mr. Tiger placidly.

A procession came around the corner. It consisted of Sylvester Wise and Marky Brown and Charlie Green. They were carrying Miss Wilson.

Behind them came Fat Olga, carrying her teacher's books.

"Here we go again!" remarked Mr. Tiger.

"Tiger! Tiger!" cried Miss Granston. "Something awful has befallen Miss Wilson. Will you not assist me? Where is your Slow Street Spirit?"

"Oh all right," said Mr. Tiger, and he turned toward the procession. "PARADE, HALT!" he shouted. "ATTEN-SHUN!"

Marky and Sylvester and Charlie all snapped to attention, and Miss Wilson fell to the floor.

"Oh look, you've dropped her," said Fat Olga.

Miss Wilson moaned softly.

"Miss Wilson! Miss Wilson! What has befallen you?" cried Miss Granston.

Miss Wilson's eyelids fluttered, and she stirred.

"Speak to me, Miss Wilson!" said Miss Granston.

Miss Wilson's lips moved feebly.

"Ug," she whispered. "Ug! Ug!" and her

head fell back on the floor, where it got a nasty bang.

"Ug?" said Miss Granston. "What *is* Ug?"

"What indeed?" said Mr. Tiger philosophically.

"Two of my Staff laid low!" said Miss Granston. "A new girl-shaped door to the Girls' Cloakroom. A hole in the school fence, a bent lamppost . . .

"And an oil slick in the road," said Miss Ash, who had slithered on it.

"What shall I do?" wailed Miss Granston.

"Send for reinforcements," said Mr. Tiger. "You know and I know that Harriet's behind this, somehow. She's got to be. And you know and I know that we aren't going to take on sorting it out single-handedly. There's only one person foolish enough to do that."

"Mr. Cousins!" gasped Miss Granston. "The Substitute Teacher Who Knows No Fear!"

"Right," said Mr. Tiger, and they sent for Mr. Cousins.

5 | Sylvester Solves It

"Here they come!" hissed Fat Olga. ·

The Anti-Harriet League took up Defensive Positions, crouching behind their desks.

Click-click-click.

"Peep."

The door of P7 swung open, and Anthea came in. Behind her came Harriet, and behind her, Dolly.

Left, right, left, right, left, right. Harriet marched down the center of the class.

Left, right, left, right, left, right. Dolly marched after her, exactly in step, but clicking with each move.

51

Harriet sat down at her desk, and Dolly sat down at the desk behind it. The only trouble was, Budgie Watts had been sitting there first.

"Hey! Get off!" said Budgie.

"*Peep-Peep-Peep-Peep-Peep.*"

"Ug," said Dolly, as she picked up Budgie by the back of the collar. She carried him down the aisle and dropped him at an empty desk, beside Walter Bruce.

"*Peep. Peep.*"

Dolly shambled, clicking, back to Budgie's desk, and sat down.

Everybody had stopped talking. They all stared at Dolly.

"Harriet?" Anthea said softly.

"Yes?" said Harriet.

"Harriet, she's *ticking*," said Anthea.

"Oh bother!" said Harriet.

"Not just ticking, Harriet," whispered Anthea. "Tick-tocking, like a clock."

"An alarm clock?" said Harriet, who knew exactly what was inside Dolly.

"Right!" said Anthea.

The classroom door opened, just a little.

It didn't open much because Miss Granston was on the other side of it, and she never opened the door of P7 wide, knowing that Harriet was inside.

"P7?" she said.

"Yes, Miss Granston!" said most of P7. *One* girl said "Ug," but Miss Granston didn't hear it, or if she did, she pretended that she didn't, for reasons of self-preservation.

"Miss Wilson is indisposed again, P7," announced Miss Granston, through the crack in the doorway. "A Substitute Teacher is on his way. The Class Monitor will take control."

And she slammed the door tight, before anyone could get at her.

There was a long silence.

"That's me," said Sylvester Wise doubtfully. Then he looked around to see what Harriet was doing. Sylvester was trapped. He knew that he was supposed to take control, but he didn't know what Harriet was planning to do about it. She had to be planning something.

But Harriet just sat quietly at her desk, with her arms folded.

"Okay, Sylvester," she said. "Get on with it!"

"On with what?" said Sylvester.

"Math," said Harriet. "We're supposed to do math, right?"

"Ug," said Dolly, in agreement.

Too surprised to wonder what Harriet was up to, Sylvester went to the teacher's desk, and got out the math book and the answer book.

"Lots of really hard problems, Sylvester," said Harriet. "None of the easy ones."

"Right!" said Sylvester, seeing his chance. "You've asked for it!"

And he put up on the blackboard all the biggest, longest, hardest problems he could find, twenty of them.

"We can't do those, Sylvester!" wailed Fat Olga. "They're much too difficult."

"I'm Class Monitor, and I'm in charge, and you're doing them!" said Sylvester.

"Let's get on with it then!" said Harriet.

Everybody started working.

Dolly clicked loudly, so loudly that it almost drowned out her ticking.

"Finished!" said Harriet.

"What?" said Sylvester.

"All the problems. I've finished. Too bad there weren't any difficult ones."

"Don't be silly!" said Sylvester bravely. "You can't have finished. You can't do math, not even simple problems. And these are Great Big Ones. . . ."

"That's what you think," said Harriet proudly.

Sylvester took a deep breath. "What's the answer to number one, then?" he said.

"5,398 centimeters," said Harriet.

Sylvester's jaw dropped.

"Number two is 978.01111," said Harriet.

"Gosh!" said Sylvester.

"Number three is 432 loaves of bread, 663 onions, and 44 cartons of milk," said Harriet.

Sylvester went pale.

"Number four is 11,831 squared," said Harriet.

"You copied!" said Sylvester. "You *must* have copied from the answer book. You know you can't do math."

"Nobody could do *this* math," muttered Fat Olga.

"Are you calling me a copycat, Sylvester?" said Harriet.

She took out her whistle.

"*Peep. Peep.*"

Dolly lumbered up from her desk.

"Sit down!" ordered Sylvester. "I said, sit down!"

But still Dolly clicked toward him . . . .

* * *

"Good afternoon, P7!" said Mr. Cousins, putting his head around the door. "All quiet and working, I see!"

"Yes, sir," said Harriet.

"I thought Wise was Class Monitor?" said Mr. Cousins.

"Sylvester let me be, sir," said Harriet. "After I got all my math right."

"Did you?" said Mr. Cousins. "Well done, Harriet!" He came into the room, and looked around him.

"Wise?" he said. "What are you doing on top of the supply closet, Wise?"

"I . . . er . . . got up here, sir," said Sylvester.

"What for, Wise?" asked Mr. Cousins, looking around him. "Brown . . . why are you crying? Green . . . ? Olga . . . ?"

Charlie Green was at his desk, but upside down, with his feet in the air.

Fat Olga was at her desk, too, but with her bookbag over her head.

"What's the meaning of this, class?" said Mr. Cousins.

Charlie and Sylvester and Marky opened their mouths to tell him.

"Ug," said Dolly menacingly.

Charlie and Sylvester and Marky closed their mouths again.

Fat Olga did say *something*, but since her head was in her bookbag, nobody heard her.

"I got all my spelling right, too, sir," said Harriet. "I expect that that is what's upset them!"

"Well, Cousins, survive Harriet and P7?" asked Mr. Tiger, when they met in the Staff Room at lunchtime.

"There's a new girl who ticks," said Mr. Cousins.

"I can believe anything of P7," said Mr. Tiger.

"Yes, but . . ." said Mr. Cousins.

"But what?"

"She also dinged twelve times, at twelve o'clock precisely."

"Amazing," said Mr. Tiger.

"And she got all her math right!" said Mr. Cousins dramatically. "*All* her math, and *all* her spelling, and *all* her vocabulary."

"Not in P7," said Mr. Tiger firmly. "I

don't believe it. Not in Harriet's class. They never do."

"She did!" said Mr. Cousins, getting excited. "She did! She did! She got every single thing right . . . AND SO DID HARRIET!"

Mr. Tiger thought about it.

"Sounds like an Educational Breakthrough!" he said.

"I can't account for it," said Mr. Cousins modestly. Actually, he thought it was because he was a much better teacher than anybody else at Slow Street, but he didn't like to say so.

The Anti-Harriet League were holed up behind the Soda Shop, having an Emergency Meeting.

"She dings!" said Sylvester. He was deep in thought. "She dings and ticks and clicks. . . ."

"And BONGS!" said Charlie, who had been bonged, so he knew all about it.

"She *clicks* when she *walks*," said Sylvester.

59

"Like a Robot," said Marky.

"A *Robot?*" said Sylvester slowly.

"She doesn't look like a Robot," said Fat Olga. "She just looks like a big girl."

"Big girls don't tick."

"Big girls don't ding!"

"Or send Morse Code signals," said Fat Olga.

"Morse Code signals?" said Sylvester.

"You couldn't see, because you were being Class Monitor," said Fat Olga. "But I could. Right through math the little green button on her sleeve kept flashing on and off, just like Morse Code signals."

"Who to?" said Charlie.

"Who-do-you-think-to?"said Fat Olga.

"Marky's right," said Sylvester darkly. "A big girl who dings and clicks and bongs and sends Morse Code signals with a little green button. And Harriet getting all her math right. She IS!"

"Is what?" said Fat Olga.

"A Robot!" said Sylvester. "Wait and see! I'll prove it!"

*   *   *

"Spaghetti *again*," said Harriet, looking at her school lunch.

"Yeugh!" said Anthea. She didn't buy school lunches. She brought her own neat lunches, in her own school lunch box.

"Ug," said the Robot.

"Eat up, Dolly!" said Harriet, and she *peeped* for the Copy Mode.

Dolly ate her lunch.

She was very quick, because she didn't have to *chew*. She just swallowed.

She was finished first, so she began again.

"Hey! That's my lunch!" said Sally Foster.

"Ug!" said Dolly, and ate it.

And another.

And another.

And another.

Twelve school lunches, one after the other.

Lots of people started shouting, but Dolly just said, "Ug," and went on eating.

"*Peeep*," went Harriet.

Dolly stopped.

"*Burp!*" went Dolly.

"Pardon," said Anthea politely.

61

"*Burp! Burp!*" went Dolly.

"How *rude!*" said Anthea.

Harriet and Anthea went out of the dining hall, with Dolly burping and clicking and ticking and dinging behind them.

"This has got to stop, Harriet," said Anthea. "I don't think my Mum will let me keep Dolly if she makes such rude noises."

"Oiling time!" said Harriet.

"There's going to be trouble, Harriet," said Anthea, as they headed for the boiler room, past the locker in the corridor.

"Sylvester *knows*, Harriet," Anthea added.

"How could he?" said Harriet.

"You got your math right," said Anthea. "And your spelling. You *know* you can't spell for beans. And Sylvester knows it, too. So he must know about Dolly."

"I bet he doesn't," said Harriet. "Sylvester's stupid."

The locker stirred, rocking angrily to and fro, but Harriet and Anthea didn't notice.

"If he doesn't know by now, he'll soon work it out," said Anthea glumly. "You know he will."

"So what?" said Harriet.

Anthea didn't know what, but she knew that Sylvester would do *something*.

The door of the boiler room closed behind them and, moments later, the door of the locker opened.

A very squashed Sylvester squeezed himself out, grinning from ear to ear.

He went off to buy a whistle.

6 | Sylvester's Revenge

Harriet and Anthea and Dolly were out in the playground playing catch.

"Watch this!" whispered Sylvester, taking a new whistle from his pocket.

The ball came straight toward Dolly.

"*Peep. Peep.*"

She swallowed it.

"Oh Dolly!" said Anthea crossly. "That's my ball."

"It was, you mean," Sylvester muttered gleefully.

Harriet and Anthea and Dolly went over to the bike shed, arguing about the Copy Mode.

"There's something wrong, Harriet," said Anthea. "She shouldn't have swallowed my ball. Not after all those lunches."

"Only twelve," said Harriet.

"I don't know where she puts it all!" said Anthea. "Twelve plates of spaghetti, and now my ball. . . ."

Harriet knew where Dolly put it, but she wasn't sure about getting it out again.

"Let's ride bikes!" she said.

"Not me," said Anthea.

"Like this, Dolly," said Harriet, and she climbed on Charlie Green's bike.

"*Peep-peep-peeeeep!*" went Harriet's whistle.

Dolly climbed on Hetty Snow's bike.

"See, Anthea?" Harriet said happily. "It's working like a charm."

Off they went.

"*Peep, peep,*" went Sylvester's whistle.

Dolly swerved, and headed straight for the kitchen door, just as the Cook was coming through it with the leftovers.

C-R-A-S-H!

"Oh brilliant, Sylvester!" breathed Fat

Olga, as Harriet and Anthea peeled the Cook
and Dolly and the bicycle out of the leftovers.

"Let me have the next turn!" said Charlie
Green. He crept over toward the bike shed,
where Harriet and Anthea were washing off
tomato sauce and pulling off strings of spaghetti.

"*Peep-Peep,*" went Charlie.

Dolly stirred, and put her hands on the
faucet. She ripped it off the pipe.

WOOOOOSH!

Water. Water *everywhere.*

"Run for it!" said Harriet. She grabbed
Dolly by one arm, while Anthea grabbed
the other, and they made their escape.

"You know what I think, Harriet?" Anthea panted. "I think Dolly is out of control!"

"Nonsense," said Harriet. "It's just a malfunction!"

"Or else somebody's *doing* it, Harriet,"
said Anthea. "Someone's fooling with my
Birthday Surprise."

"Like who?" said Harriet.

"Like Sylvester," said Anthea.

"Sylvester isn't smart enough," said Harriet, and they went to dry off and get changed for Gym.

"Sir! Sir!" said Sylvester, catching up with Mr. Cousins outside the Gym.

"Yes, Wise?" said Mr. Cousins.

"We got you a present, sir," said Sylvester. "For being our Substitute Teacher, sir. It's a whistle, sir. For Gym, sir."

"Well, thank you very much, Sylvester," said Mr. Cousins. "You and all your little friends who . . . er . . . contributed."

"Think nothing of it, sir," chorused the Anti-Harriet League.

The cost of the whistle was money well spent, from the point of view of the League. It could destroy Harriet forever!

7 | The Robot's Rampage

P7 were in the Gym.

It was hard work for Harriet, because she had to keep *peeping* her whistle, to show Dolly what to do.

But it was worth it. Dolly was *brilliant!*

Nobody else could lift all the dumbbells one handed.

Even Charlie Green couldn't do 394 handstands, one after the other.

"At least three meters over the pommel horse!" said Mr. Cousins, scratching his head in amazement. Then he had to pick Fat Olga up, because Dolly had landed on her. Fat

Olga made a soft landing place but lost a lot of air.

"Well done, Dolly," said Anthea happily. She was already planning a Big Welcome-Dolly Tea Party for when they got home. This was her best Birthday Surprise ever!

"Aerobic Exercises!" said Mr. Cousins, switching on the taped music. "And we'll let our new girl lead."

"Oh dear!" said Anthea.

"Sir . . ." began Harriet.

"Ready, steady, go!" said Mr. Cousins.

"Tum-tum-tum-tum-tee-tum-tum-tum!" went the music.

"*Peep-peeep-peep*," went Harriet uncertainly.

Dolly wavered. Then she shot one leg up in the air behind her, and started hopping on the other one.

"One leg, everybody!" Mr. Cousins shouted. "After her!"

P7 hopped by, with Dolly in the lead.

Once around the Gym. Twice. Thrice. Four times. Five times. Six times. Seven times. Eight times . . .

"Stop her, Harriet!" panted Anthea, who had short legs, and wasn't much of a hopper.

"*Peep! Peeep!*" went Harriet.

Dolly wavered, in midhop, and tried to change legs.

C-R-A-S-H!

Over went the Robot.

And over went everybody else.

" 'A' for Effort, P7!" cried Mr. Cousins. "As a reward, let's play Basketball!"

"Oh dear," said Anthea.

Sylvester glowed. His Hour had come. "Sir! Sir!" he shouted. "We have to let the new girl play. She's the best jumper I've ever seen, sir!"

"You're right!" said Mr. Cousins.

"And don't forget to use your new whistle, sir," said Fat Olga cunningly.

"I certainly won't, Olga," said Mr. Cousins.

"Now *peep* your way out of that, Harriet!" muttered Sylvester, as the two teams lined up.

"Harriet!" Anthea said despairingly, as Mr. Cousins put his new whistle to his lips.

"Don't worry," said Harriet. "Copy Mode! She'll copy the others. No problem!"

Marky Brown and Douglas Rose and Mandy Smallwood and Fat Olga were on Olga's team. Sylvester and Dolly and Anthea and Freddie Hill were on Sylvester's. The rest of the class hung on the bars.

Harriet blew her whistle for the Copy Mode.

"*Peep.*"

Mr. Cousins blew his whistle to begin the game. It was a mistake, but he didn't know it.

"*Peeep!*"

Click-click-click (with an occasional tick) went Dolly.

She clicked up to Mandy Smallwood.

"Go away, you!" said Mandy.

"Ug?" said Dolly, not very sure what to do next.

Harriet blew her whistle furiously, but Mr. Cousins blew his whistle at the same time and her *peep-peep* blended with Mr. Cousin's *peep*, to give a new and confusing sound.

Dolly stopped. She stood there, clicking, and then something inside her computer brain went *CLUNK!* and stuck, in the Copy Mode.

Dolly clicked around, to see what the others were doing, so that she could copy it.

They were throwing things into a little net, at one end of the Gym, so Dolly picked up the nearest thing, too, which happened to be Mandy Smallwood.

"Oh! Leggo!" shrieked Mandy.

"*Peep!*" went Mr. Cousins, but Dolly wasn't paying any attention, now that her brain had gotten stuck.

Click-click-click she went, ambling up the Gym, as Fat Olga's team got out of her way.

She arrived beneath the basketball net. *Click!* She steadied herself.

Then . . .

> *click-click-click*

. . . up went Mandy Smallwood in the air. Down she came again, but not in the net.

"Missed!" said Sylvester cheerfully. "No basket!"

Peeep! Mr. Cousins ran down the Gym, blowing briskly on his whistle.

Dolly heard the *peep!* clearly this time and turned sharply.

Her long arms reached out for the on-rushing Mr. Cousins and plucked him off his feet.

Before he knew what was happening, Mr. Cousins was soaring through the air.

"H-E-L-P!" he cried.

He came down in the net, with his bottom firmly stuck where the ball should be.

"Score!" yelled Harriet enthusiastically.

"Doesn't count!" said Sylvester.

"*Harriet*," wailed Anthea.

Mr. Cousins wrenched and wriggled and ripped.

The ripping was his trousers, which had split down the middle. Mr. Cousins stopped wrenching and wriggling at once, and turned red instead. He opened his mouth to gasp, and swallowed his whistle.

"*Wheep! Wheep!*" went the whistle inside him.

CLUNK-CLUNK went something inside Dolly's computer brain, as she picked up the fresh signal.

"*Peep-peep-peep*," went Harriet's whistle.

"Oh dear!" went Anthea.

Dolly stopped, wavered, gave a little whir, and took off!

ZOOOOOOOOOOOOOOOOOOOOM!

CRASH!

SMASH!

BANG!

WALLOP!

CRUNCH!

The *Zoom* was Dolly Zooming.

The *Crash* was when she went through the Gym doors, without bothering to open them.

The *Smash* was when she bounced off Mr. Tiger, who was having a quiet pipe behind the P6 Aeronautics Display in the corridor.

The *Bang* was when she hit the wall of P6, and the *Wallop* was when she came right out the other side, into the playground.

The *Crunch* was when the rest of the wall fell on P6.

It was quiet after that.

At least, it was quiet *inside* Slow Street School. There was quite a lot of noise *outside* it.

The noise was caused by Dolly, hopping

down Main Street, still clicking and ticking.

"Dolly! Big Dolly! Come Back!" Anthea cried, in hot pursuit.

"*Peep-peep-peeep!*" went Harriet despairingly, but her *peeps* were drowned by the howl of police sirens and the wail of fire engines headed toward Slow Street School.

Dolly's trail stopped at the canal, which was deep and dark and muddy, and wider than even Dolly's best jump.

"Oh no!" cried Anthea. "Not my Dolly!"

"She was only a Robot after all," Harriet pointed out sensibly. "I'll make you another one, Anthea."

"Another one won't be the same!" said Anthea. "I want my Dolly." But Dolly was nowhere to be found.

Finally Harriet and Anthea went back to school — or what was left of it.

Anthea sniffled right through the last class. Then they started home.

"Anthea!" gasped Harriet. "Look!"

There was a trail of muddy footprints down Harriet's drive, leading to the garage.

"Dolly! Big Dolly!" shrieked Anthea.

Dolly was in the garage. Or at least a great big pile of mud with a muddy thumb stuck in its mouth was there, draped over Mr. Smith's little car.

"*Peep-peep-peep!*" went Harriet.

"I think you'd better not do that, Harriet," said Anthea anxiously.

"But I want to make her work again!" said Harriet.

"I love her just the way she is," said Anthea. "She's perfect! She's my Dolly, and she's coming home to my house and she's going to live with me forever."

"Better give her a bath first," said Harriet, and they did.

That was how Dolly came to be standing in the corner of Anthea's playroom, in a nice clean uniform, with her hair all shiny from Lavender Shampoo, when Anthea said good night to her.

"My very best Surprise Birthday Present ever!" said Anthea, and she kissed Dolly good night, and went up the stairs.

Dolly was still a bit damp, but Anthea had put her by the radiator.

As the evening wore on, Dolly dried off.

By eleven o'clock, when Anthea's Dad took Fido for a walk, Dolly was completely dry.

"*Peep-peep-peep*," went Anthea's Dad, on his special dog whistle.

In the darkness of Anthea's playroom, something stirred, and clicked, and moved. . . .